TACKLE 22

By Louise Munro Foley

Illustrated by John Heinly

A Yearling Book

for Mom and Dad

Published by
Dell Publishing Co., Inc.
1 Dag Hammarskjold Plaza
New York, New York 10017

Text copyright © 1978 by Louise Munro Foley

Illustrations copyright © 1978 by John Heinly

Yearling ® TM 913705, Dell Publishing Co., Inc.

ISBN: 0-440-48484-7

Reprinted by arrangement with Delacorte Press

Printed in the United States of America

Second Dell Printing—November 1982
CW

"Rats!" said Lenny. "Rats, rats, rats." He hung up the phone and looked sadly at Willy and Chub. "Bad news, Wildcats. Steve has the mumps."

"MUMPS?" yelled Willy. "He can't! We have a game on Saturday! The play-off! Wildcats versus Spacemen!"

Lenny sighed. "Had a game, you mean. Without Steve, we don't have a quarterback. Without a quarterback, we don't have a team. Without a team..."

Willy nodded. "No game," he said.

"It's just not fair," said Chub. "This has been our best season ever, and now we have to forfeit the big one."

Every Saturday the Wildcats and the Spacemen had played football in the vacant lot at the end of the street. Now the football season was ending and they were tied at five games each.

"We better tell them," said Lenny.

"Yeah," said Chub. "Game canceled—mumps."

The three boys walked slowly down the street to the lot. When they got there, the Spacemen were in a huddle.

"Get the Wildcats!" they yelled. "14—39—6! The Spacemen are champs!"

"Just look at them," said Willy, sadly. "They look like pros."

The four Spacemen had bought new green jerseys for the play-off game.

"Boy," said Chub. "I wish we had new uniforms."

"Well, I wish we had another player," muttered Lenny.

As they got closer, one of the Spacemen yelled, "Hey, Wildcats! We heard about your quarterback. Did you come to forfeit the game?"

Lenny curled his hands into fists.

"You dumb Spacemen!" he shouted. "The Wildcats are going to play on Saturday, Steve or no Steve! We're going to put you in orbit!"

"Right," hollered Willy.

"Wildcats, Wildcats, four in a row!... Wildcats, Wildcats, go—go—GO!"

The Spacemen just laughed.

"Don't you mean three in a row?" asked
their quarterback. "You can't even count!"
"They're not Wildcats," said another
Spaceman. "They're the three little kittens!"

Lenny was furious. He ran toward the Spacemen. As he was about to tackle the quarterback, Willy and Chub grabbed him and pulled him out of the lot.

They were still trying to calm him down when they met Chub's little brother Herbie.

Well, Herbie wasn't exactly little. He was younger than Chub but big for his age.

"Hi, Chub," Herbie said. "Where are you going?"

"None of your business," Chub answered. "Get lost, Herbie."

"But Mom said you have to play with me."

"Just what I need," Chub said. "Steve's got the mumps, the Spacemen are laughing at us, and now I have to baby-sit for you."

The boys started down the street. Herbie tagged along behind.

"Hey, Chub!" he said. "Can I take Steve's place?"

"What?" replied Chub. He didn't even turn around.

"I can play football," said Herbie.

"You're too little," said Chub.

"Am not."

"Are too."

"Hey, Chub!" Herbie yelled after his brother. "I am a GOOD football player.

"Look! I can be a RUSHER!"

He started to run. His head was down and his arms were out.

Chub had no warning at all. Herbie jumped. His arms grabbed Chub's waist and his feet wrapped around Chub's legs.

SPLOOSH!

They both landed in a muddy flower bed.

"Dimwit," muttered Chub. "Lamebrain. Dummy."

He pulled himself out of the mud and glared at his little brother.

Willy and Lenny were laughing.

"Good tackle, Herbie," said Lenny.

"Yeah," giggled Willy. "Super!"

Herbie grinned. "Can I play on Saturday?" he asked.

Willy and Lenny nodded.

Chub scowled. He was outvoted and he knew it.

"Oh, all right," he said. "Let's go to the locker room."

The locker room was really Lenny's garage. The Wildcats kept their equipment there. Everything was in a big box marked:

IMPORTANT
KEEP OUT!!
(this means YOU.)

In the box there were old football magazines, torn shirts, and some battered helmets.

"I wish we had new jerseys like the Spacemen," said Lenny. He threw a shirt at Herbie. "See how this fits," he said.

"Wow. Number 22," said Herbie. "That's my lucky number!"

He put on the shirt. It hung down past his hips, and the sleeves covered his hands. "Perfect!" said Herbie.

He reached for a helmet and plopped it down on his head. It covered his eyes and half of his nose.

"Perfect!" yelled Herbie, jumping up and down.

The boys practiced every day after school.

Lenny tried to be patient with Herbie, but it was difficult.

When Lenny told Herbie to pass to the left, Herbie would pass to the right. When Lenny told him to run the ball down the middle, Herbie would run out of bounds.

The only thing Herbie did well was tackle.

Herbie tackled everything that moved and some things that didn't.

On Wednesday he tackled O'Reilly's dog.
(That was noisy.)

On Thursday he tackled the garbage can.
(That was a mess.)

And on Friday he tackled a tree. (That was almost the end of his tackling career.)

Chub and Willy called him "The Mad Rusher," but Lenny didn't think Herbie was funny. Lenny took football very seriously.

On the day Herbie tackled the tree, Lenny got angry.

"It's not funny!" he yelled at Herbie. "There's more to football than tackling. You've got to know how to pass and kick and run and... Herbie! You're going to lose this game for us!"

Herbie stared at Lenny. He was confused, and sore, and most of all he was tired of having Lenny tell him about all the things he did wrong.

Herbie started to cry. "Quit pickin' on me," he said to Lenny. And he snatched up his helmet and ran home.

Then Chub got mad. "That's right," he yelled. "Quit pickin' on my brother!" And Chub ran off after Herbie.

"I didn't mean to hurt his feelings," Lenny mumbled.

"Maybe you didn't mean to," said Willy. "But you did." And he walked away and left Lenny standing alone in the vacant lot.

When Lenny got home, he went straight to his room and flopped on the bed. He felt terrible.

"What's the matter, Len?" It was his older brother, Tom.

Lenny began to cry. "Herbie can't do anything right," he said. "And everybody sticks up for him. They all think he's funny, but he's going to make us lose the play-off tomorrow. I just know it!" He punched his hand into his pillow.

"Look," said Tom. "There are only three rules that Herbie needs to remember. Rule One: When the Spacemen have the ball, tackle the man with the ball. Rule Two: When the Wildcats have the ball, keep the Spacemen away from it. And Rule Three: Play just as hard when you're ahead as you do when you're behind—some pretty big teams have had problems remembering that one."

"You mean that's all I need to tell Herbie? No pass patterns? None of that stuff?"

"No, that's not important now," Tom replied.

"Well," said Lenny, "if you say so."

But he was still worried. That night, Lenny wore his Wildcat jersey to bed, for luck.

On Saturday before the game, the boys met at the locker room.

"I've got something to say," Lenny announced. He looked down at the floor. "I'm sorry about yesterday."

"That's okay," said Chub. "No hard feelings."

"Yeah," said Herbie. "I guess I don't know many football rules."

"That's just it," said Lenny. "You don't have to."

And he told them Tom's three rules.

"That's all?" Herbie asked.

"That's all, Herb," said Lenny.

Herbie grinned. No one had ever called him "Herb" before!

"Well," he hollered, "if that's all we need to know—let's go get those Spacemen!"

When they arrived at the lot, the Spacemen were already there.

The Wildcats got into a huddle.

"Now, remember the rules," said Lenny nervously.

"Right," Herbie replied. He pushed his helmet up so he could see.

"Come on, Wildcats. We're going to win today!" yelled Willy.

"You bet!" said Lenny. But he really wasn't sure.

Chub pulled a clock from his pocket, set the alarm for thirty minutes, and put the clock on a tree stump.

Then the Spacemen and the Wildcats ran out on the field.

The Spacemen kicked off, but Chub
fumbled the ball and the Spacemen recovered.
"It's okay, Chub," said Herbie. "Don't
worry. Things will get better."
But they didn't.

Two plays later, the Spacemen scored the first touchdown.

"Block for me, Wildcats," yelled Lenny.
"Let's get that touchdown back right now!"

The Spacemen lined up for the kickoff.

The football sailed down the center of the field. Lenny grabbed the ball and ran toward the goal posts. He didn't look to the right and he didn't look to the left. He knew the Wildcats were blocking for him.

And Lenny tied the score!
But at halftime, the game was still tied:

SPACEMEN—6 : WILDCATS—6

"Oh, wow," panted Lenny as he collapsed under a tree. "Wildcats! We've got to get out there and win!"

When the second half started, the Spacemen had the ball.

"Get him, Herbie," the Wildcats yelled.

Herbie took off. His head was down. His arms were out.

POW!

Herbie and the Spaceman went down in the dirt. The ball went up in the air. Lenny grabbed it and went racing down the field. The Spacemen ran after him, but they didn't catch him!

Lenny scored!

"Hold that lead!" Lenny yelled, dancing up and down.

Both teams played as hard as they could after that, but neither team scored. The Wildcats were still ahead.

Then with only three minutes to go, Willie fumbled a pass. One of the Spacemen grabbed the ball and ran.

Herbie pushed up his helmet so he could see.

The Spacemen were going to score!

There was only one thing for Herbie to
do. He took off. His head was down. His
arms were out.

POW!

Herbie tackled the Spaceman just before
he crossed the goal line.

Suddenly the alarm went off.
The game was over.
The Wildcats had won!

The boys danced and hugged each other
as they gave the Wildcat yell:

"Wildcats, Wildcats, four in a row!...
Wildcats, Wildcats, go—go—GO!"

"Next year," hollered Lenny, "we'll be
FIVE in a row...because Herb's going to be
on this team permanently!"

Herbie pushed his helmet up and grinned.
"When do we start practicing?" he asked.

MS READ-a-thon—
a simple way to start youngsters reading

Boys and girls between 6 and 14 can join the MS READ-a-thon and help find a cure for Multiple Sclerosis by reading books. And they get two rewards — the enjoyment of reading, and the great feeling that comes from helping others.

Parents and educators: For complete information call your local MS chapter. Or mail the coupon below.

Kids can help, too!

Mail to:
National Multiple Sclerosis Society
205 East 42nd Street
New York, N.Y. 10017

I would like more information about the MS READ-a-thon and how it can work in my area.

MS
Mystery
Sleuth
™

Name _____
(please print)

Address _____

City _____ State _____ Zip _____

Organization _____

1—80